PEDRO

PEDRO'S MONSTER

by Fran Manushkin

illustrated by
Tammie Lyon

PICTURE WINDOW BOOKS
a capstone imprint

Pedro is published by Picture Window Books,
A Capstone Imprint
1710 Roe Crest Drive
North Mankato, Minnesota 56003
www.capstonepub.com

Text © 2019 Fran Manushkin
Illustrations © 2019 Picture Window Books

Library of Congress Cataloging-in-Publication Data
Names: Manushkin, Fran, author. | Lyon, Tammie, illustrator.
Title: Pedro's monster / by Fran Manushkin ; illustrated by Tammie Lyon.
Description: North Mankato, Minnesota : Picture Window Books, [2018] |
    Series: Pedro | Summary: Despite his father's reassurances, Pedro is
    frightened by the monsters in his dreams—until he finds a way to use his
    love of monster trucks to defeat his dream monsters.
Identifiers: LCCN 2018002733 (print) | LCCN 2018004451 (ebook) |
    ISBN 9781515828372 (eBook pdf) | ISBN 9781515828211 (hardcover) |
    ISBN 9781515828266 (pbk.)
Subjects: LCSH: Hispanic American boys—Juvenile fiction. | Dreams—Juvenile
    fiction. | Fear—Juvenile fiction. | Monster trucks—Juvenile fiction. |
    CYAC: Monster trucks—Fiction. | Trucks—Fiction. | Monsters—Fiction. |
    Dreams—Fiction. | Fear—Fiction. | Hispanic Americans—Fiction.
Classification: LCC PZ7.M3195 (ebook) | LCC PZ7.M3195 Pcm 2018 (print) | DDC
    813.54 [E]—dc23
LC record available at https://lccn.loc.gov/2018002733

Designer: Kayla Rossow
Design Elements by Shutterstock

Printed and bound in the USA
PA021

Table of Contents

Chapter 1
Bad Dreams

Pedro was dreaming.

He dreamed that a creepy

green dragon was chasing

him. The dragon was blowing

flames!

Pedro told his dad about

his dream.

His dad said, "Don't worry

about it. Dream dragons can't

hurt you."

Pedro tried to forget his dream. He raced his trucks all over the yard.

He and his brother Paco did speedy donuts, going around and around. They got nice and dizzy.

Pedro told Paco, "Now I'll

jump over the highest hill."

Oops! Pedro went flying

and landed in the mud.

"Cool!" he yelled.

The next night, Pedro

had another bad dream. He

dreamed that a long slimy

worm was creeping up his leg!

Pedro's dad told him,

"Dream worms cannot hurt

you. And I have a nice surprise.

I'm taking you and your friends

to a monster truck rally."

"Yay!" yelled Pedro. "Cool!"

Pedro and Katie and JoJo

painted posters for the rally.

BASH AND SMASH!

MASH AND SMASH!

CRUSH! CRUSH! CRUSH!

They were ready to cheer

on the truck drivers.

Chapter 2
Rally Time

The next day was the

rally. The first truck did a

somersault and landed in

the mud. *THUD! SPLASH!*

"Awesome!" Pedro yelled.

"I did that too."

A gigantic school bus

crushed three cars!

"I'd like to drive that,"

shouted Katie.

JoJo smiled. "You *would!*"

The trucks were fierce,

roaring and doing wheelies

around each other.

"Super awesome!" yelled

Pedro.

The next day at school, Pedro wrote a story about monster trucks. He could not stop thinking about them.

But Pedro kept having bad

dreams. Each night before

bedtime, Pedro ate cookies,

hoping to have sweet dreams.

He didn't.

Each day after school,

Pedro raced his trucks. He

went faster and roared louder.

"Go, BIG THUNDER!"

cheered Katie.

"That's you!" shouted JoJo.

"BIG THUNDER!"

"Right!" yelled Pedro. "I am noisy, and I am fast! Nothing can stop me."

Pedro kept smiling. He smiled all through dinner.

Chapter 3
Big Thunder

That night at bedtime, Pedro told himself, "I am strong! I am powerful! I am BIG THUNDER!"

Pedro said it again and again until he fell asleep.

Then it happened!

Pedro had a horrible

dream. That creepy green

dragon began chasing him!

The dragon roared and blew

his scary flames!

But Pedro didn't run away. He roared back—loud as thunder. Pedro chased that dragon around in circles and into the mud!

The dragon's fire went out!

He cried and cried, saying,

"You are so fierce!"

Then he ran away.

Katie and JoJo cheered,

"Way to go, BIG THUNDER!"

Pedro woke up smiling.

He told his mom and dad

about his dream.

"You were great, Pedro!"

said his mom.

"Way to go!" said his dad.

Pedro couldn't stop smiling.

"You were right," he told his dad. "Dream monsters cannot hurt me."

Then Pedro gobbled up his breakfast—Chocolate Crunch!

About the Author

Fran Manushkin is the author of
many popular picture books, including
Happy in Our Skin; *Baby, Come Out!*;
*Latkes and Applesauce: A Hanukkah
Story*; *The Tushy Book*; *Big Girl
Panties*; *Big Boy Underpants*; and
Bamboo for Me, Bamboo for You!
There is a real Katie Woo—she's Fran's great-niece—
but she never gets in half the trouble of the Katie
Woo in the books. Fran writes on her beloved Mac
computer in New York City, without the help of her
two naughty cats, Chaim and Goldy.

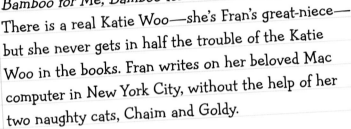

About the Illustrator

Tammie Lyon began her love for
drawing at a young age while sitting
at the kitchen table with her dad.
She continued her love of art and
eventually attended the Columbus
College of Art and Design, where
she earned a bachelor's degree in
fine art. After a brief career as
a professional ballet dancer, she
decided to devote herself full time to illustration.
Today she lives with her husband, Lee, in
Cincinnati, Ohio. Her dogs, Gus and Dudley,
keep her company as she works in her studio.

Glossary

awesome (AW-suhm)—extremely good

dizzy (DIZ-ee)—having a feeling of being unsteady or having a spinning head

donuts (DOH-nuhts)—motions that send vehicles spinning around in tight circles

fierce (FEERS)—daring and dangerous

gigantic (jye-GAN-tik)—huge

monster truck rally (MON-stur TRUHK RAL-ee)—a competition where monster trucks race and perform tricks

slimy (SLY-mee)—covered with or producing slime

somersault (SUHM-ur-sawlt)—a stunt where the back end of a monster truck rolls forward and over the top of the front end until the truck is back on its four wheels

speedy (SPEE-dee)—very fast

wheelies (WEE-lees)—a trick where the truck drives forward with its front wheels off the ground

Let's Talk

1. Describe the dreams Pedro had. Compare them with your own dreams. Have you ever had any dreams that were similar to Pedro's?

2. What things did Pedro try to do to avoid bad dreams? What finally worked?

3. Pedro gets a new nickname in this story. What is it? Explain why it is a good nickname for him.

Let's Write

1. Using the internet, look at photos of monster trucks or watch videos of them. Then write three sentences to describe monster trucks.

2. Pretend you are going to a monster truck rally and create your own poster. Be sure to include a chant or saying on the poster.

3. Draw your own monster truck, then write a paragraph about it. Be sure to include its name and what its most famous trick is.

JOKE AROUND

- Where do you get dragon milk?
  from a cow with short legs

- Why do dragons sleep during the day?
  So they can fight knights.

- Do monsters eat popcorn with
  their fingers?
  No, they eat the fingers separately.

- What's big and scary
  and has three wheels?
  a monster riding
  on a tricycle

○ What do you say
when you meet
a two-headed
monster?
"Bye-bye."

○ What's the best
way to talk to a monster?
from a long ways away

○ What kind of horses do
monsters ride?
night mares

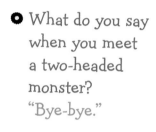

THE FUN DOESN'T STOP HERE!

Discover more at www.capstonekids.com

- Videos & Contests
- Games & Puzzles
- Friends & Favorites
- Authors & Illustrators

Find cool websites and more books like this one at www.facthound.com. Just type in the Book ID: 9781515828211 and you're ready to go!